Green Light Readers
For the new reader who's ready to GO!

Amazing adventures await every young child who is eager to read.

Green Light Readers encourage children to explore, to imagine, and to grow through books. Created for beginning readers at two levels of skill, these lively illustrated stories have been carefully developed to reinforce reading basics taught at school and to make reading a fun and rewarding experience for children and grown-ups to share outside the classroom.

The grades and ages within each skill level are general guidelines only, and books included in both levels may feature any or all of the bulleted characteristics. When choosing a book for a new reader, remember that every child progresses at his or her own pace—be patient and supportive as the magic of reading takes hold.

1 Buckle up!
Kindergarten–Grade 1: Developing reading skills, ages 5–7
- Short, simple stories • Fully illustrated • Familiar objects and situations
- Playful rhythms • Spoken language patterns of children
- Rhymes and repeated phrases • Strong link between text and art

2 Start the engine!
Grades 1–2: Reading with help, ages 6–8
- Longer stories, including nonfiction • Short chapters
- Generously illustrated • Less-familiar situations
- More fully developed characters • Creative language, including dialogue
- More subtle link between text and art

Green Light Readers incorporate characteristics detailed in the Reading Recovery model used by educators to assess the readability of texts through the end of first grade. Guidelines for reading levels for these readers have been developed with assistance from Mary Lou Meerson. An educational consultant, Ms. Meerson has been a classroom teacher, a language arts coordinator, an elementary school principal, and a university professor.

Published in collaboration with Harcourt School Publishers

Farmers Market

Farmers

Carmen Parks

Market

Illustrated by Edward Martinez

Green Light Readers
Harcourt, Inc.
San Diego   New York   London

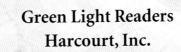

www.harcourt.com

First Green Light Readers edition 2002
Green Light Readers is a trademark of Harcourt, Inc.,
registered in the United States of America and/or other jurisdictions.

Library of Congress Cataloging-in-Publication Data
Parks, Carmen.
Farmers market/Carmen Parks; illustrated by Edward Martinez.
p. cm.
"Green Light Readers."
Summary: A girl and her parents spend the day at the farmers' market selling the vegetables they've grown.
[1. Farmers' markets—Fiction.] I. Martinez, Edward, ill. II. Title. III. Series.
PZ7.P2398Far 2002
[E]—dc21 2001002415
ISBN 0-15-216680-7
ISBN 0-15-216674-2 (pb)

A C E G H F D B
A C E G H F D B (pb)

It's still dark, but it's time for me to get up. It's market day in Red Rock.

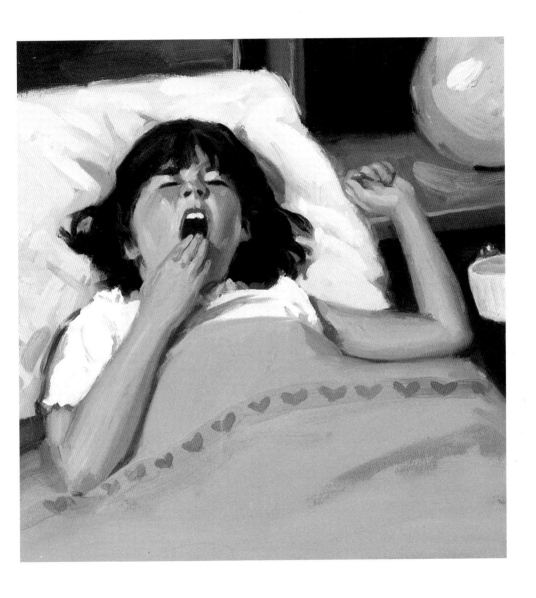

I always go to the market with Mom and Dad. We sell fruits and vegetables from our farm.

We have to get up early because
the market is far away.

As we start out this morning,
the stars are still shining.

At last we get to Red Rock. We park the truck in the big lot and then set up our cart.

We have lots of fruits and vegetables
to sell.

"This corn smells fresh," a man says.
"These eggplants look fresh, too."

Lots of people stop at our cart.
My best friend, Carmen, stops by.

Carmen fills her arms with corn.
She gets some lemons, too.

Dad sells the last of the corn.
Now, nothing is left on the cart!

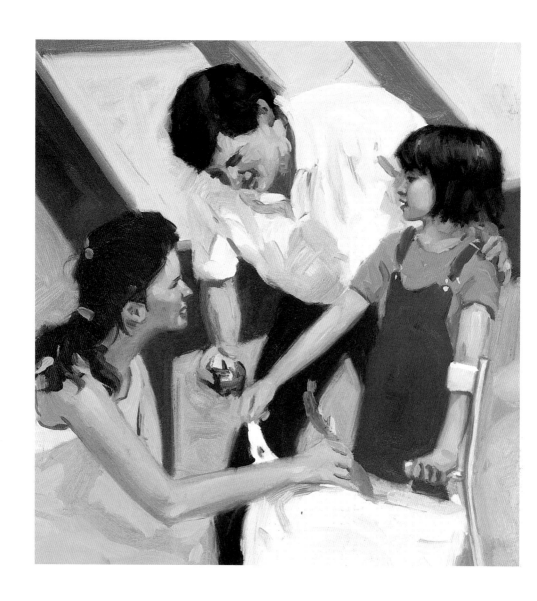

Market day is over. We pick up the trash and go back home.

Market days always go by fast.
I think I like market days the best!

Meet the Illustrator

Edward Martinez loves to paint. He began his work on Farmers Market by taking pictures of real children. Then he looked at the photos as he painted the children in the story. Look closely, the kids might be based on someone you know!

Edward Martinez

Look for these other Green Light Readers
in affordably priced paperbacks and hardcovers!

Level 2/Grades 1–2

Animals on the Go
Jessica Brett
Illustrated by Richard Cowdrey

A Bed Full of Cats
Holly Keller

Boots for Beth
Alex Moran
Illustrated by Lisa Campbell Ernst

Catch Me If You Can!
Bernard Most

The Chick That Wouldn't Hatch
Claire Daniel
Illustrated by Lisa Campbell Ernst

Daniel's Mystery Egg
Alma Flor Ada
Illustrated by G. Brian Karas

Digger Pig and the Turnip
Caron Lee Cohen
Illustrated by Christopher Denise

The Fox and the Stork
Gerald McDermott

Get That Pest!
Erin Douglas
Illustrated by Wong Herbert Yee

I Wonder
Tana Hoban

Marco's Run
Wesley Cartier
Illustrated by Reynold Ruffins

The Purple Snerd
Rozanne Lanczak Williams
Illustrated by Mary GrandPré

Shoe Town
Janet Stevens and Susan Stevens Crummel
Illustrated by Janet Stevens

Splash!
Ariane Dewey and Jose Aruego

Tumbleweed Stew
Susan Stevens Crummel
Illustrated by Janet Stevens

The Very Boastful Kangaroo
Bernard Most

Where Do Frogs Come From?
Alex Vern

Why the Frog Has Big Eyes
Betsy Franco
Illustrated by Joung Un Kim

And for younger readers, look for
Level 1/Kindergarten–Grade 1 Green Light Readers

Green Light Readers
For the new reader who's ready to GO!